Dealing With...
A NEW BABY

by Jane Lacey
Illustrated by Venitia Dean

PowerKiDS
press™

Published in 2019 by **The Rosen Publishing Group, Inc.**
29 East 21st Street, New York, NY 10010

Cataloging-in-Publication Data
Names: Lacey, Jane. | Dean, Venitia, illustrator.
Title: A new baby / Jane Lacey; illustrated by Venitia Dean.
Description: New York : PowerKids Press, 2019. | Series: Dealing with... | Includes glossary and index.
Identifiers: LCCN ISBN 9781538338957 (pbk.) | ISBN 9781538338940 (library bound) | ISBN 9781538338964 (6 pack)
Subjects: LCSH: Newborn infants--Juvenile literature. | Brothers and sisters--Juvenile literature. | Families--Juvenile literature.
Classification: LCC HQ774.L33 2019 | DDC 306.875'3--dc23

Editor: Sarah Peutrill
Series Design: Collaborate

Manufactured in the United States of America

CPSIA Compliance Information: Batch #CSPK18: For Further Information contact Rosen Publishing, New York, New York at 1-800-237-9932.

Contents

I DON'T WANT A NEW BABY!

Ellie's mom and dad are happy because they are expecting a baby. Ellie's little sister Jenny is excited, but Ellie isn't. She doesn't want a new baby in the family.

Jenny is Ellie's little sister

Our new baby is going to have my bedroom. I'm going to share my big sister Ellie's bedroom. I'm happy, but Ellie is grumpy about the baby, and she's really grumpy with me!

Jenny

Ellie's story

When Mom and Dad told Jenny and me and about the new baby, Jenny jumped up and down and said, "We're having a new baby!" over and over again. I pretended to be happy, but I'm not really. I've got to share my bedroom with Jenny. She can be a real pest! Mom, Dad, Jenny, and I all play tennis together. We won't be able to with a new baby. Babies are a nuisance! They cry and have smelly diapers. I don't think I'll love a new baby.

Ellie

What can Ellie do?

She doesn't have to pretend to be happy. She can:

★ tell her mom and dad she doesn't think she'll love the new baby
★ say she doesn't want things to change
★ say she wishes she didn't have to share a room with Jenny

What Ellie did

Mom and Dad were glad I talked to them. I think they knew how I felt already! They said it can take time to get used to a new baby, but changes can be exciting. Jenny and I are helping to decorate our room and the baby's room. We're getting bunk beds. I'm getting the top bunk!

EXPECTING A BABY

A baby grows in its mother's womb. It grows very slowly, so there is plenty of time to get ready. As the baby grows, the mother's tummy gets bigger and bigger. After about five months, you can feel the baby move and kick if you put your hand gently on the mother's bump. For the first few months, a mother sometimes feels sick. As her tummy gets bigger, she can feel uncomfortable and tired. After nine months, the baby is ready to be born.

I'M WORRIED THAT MOM AND THE BABY WON'T BE ALL RIGHT

Liam's mom is expecting a baby. His dad is looking after her extra carefully and keeps asking her if she's all right. Now Liam's worried she won't be all right.

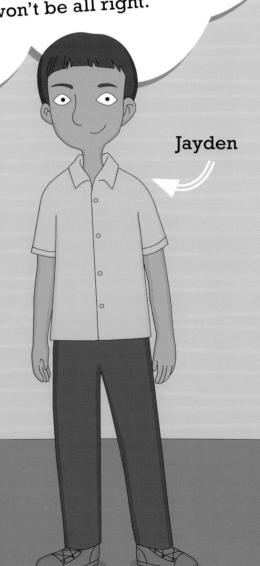

Jayden

Jayden is Liam's friend

Liam keeps asking me about when my baby sister was born. I don't know — she was just born! She was OK and Mom was OK. Why shouldn't they be? I wish he'd stop talking about it.

Mom's having a baby.
I hope it's a boy, but it might
be a girl. Jayden's baby
sister is OK, I guess.

Dad keeps fussing over
Mom as if something bad
might happen. Is something
bad going to happen? How
can I tell?

When I ask Jayden about
his mom having a baby, he
says he can't remember.
Then he says it'll be fine and
not to worry!

But I am worried. I want
Mom and the baby to be all
right.

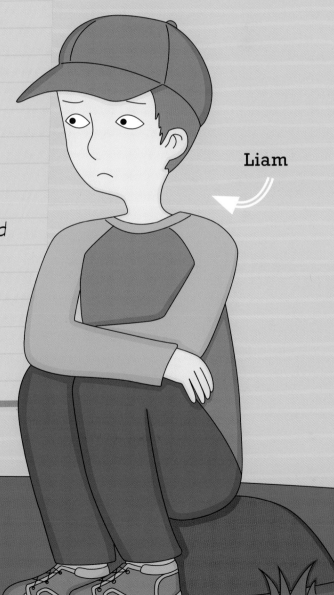

Liam

What can Liam do?

Liam is worried because he doesn't know why Dad is fussing over Mom. He can:

★ talk to his dad
★ ask him why he seems to be worried
★ say now he's feeling worried, too

What Liam did

I talked to Dad. He said I was born early. I had to stay in the hospital for weeks. He was worried it might happen again.

But now we are both worrying less. Mom and the baby are healthy. I've seen a scan of the baby. It looks like a frog!

GETTING READY FOR THE BABY

Fran was excited about having a new baby brother or sister.

First we decorated the baby's room. Then we went shopping.

We bought so much stuff, just for one tiny baby!

Mom got bigger and bigger until one day she said, "The baby's coming!"

Dad took Mom to the hospital. Gram looked after me. I made a card and got a teddy for the baby.

Dad phoned and said, "It's a girl!" I was one of the first people to see her. She made a funny face at me, but I think she likes me.

THE NEW BABY IS BORING!

Frankie was looking forward to having a baby brother to play with. But baby Charlie is too little to play. Frankie thinks he's boring.

Baby Charlie only sleeps, eats, cries, and has smelly diapers. Sometimes he just does nothing. Mom and Dad expect me to play with him, but there's no point. I'll wait until he's old enough.

Frankie's story

Charlie

Frankie

What can Frankie do?

There are lots of things Frankie can do for baby Charlie. He can:

* help dress, bathe, and burp him
* hold him carefully when he's sitting down
* help push his stroller when they go out for a walk
* talk to him, tell him stories, and sing to him

Baby Charlie will soon get to know him. Frankie might be the first person he smiles at. Soon Frankie will be able to make baby Charlie laugh.

It won't be long before they are good friends.

13

I'M JEALOUS OF THE NEW BABY

Mia knows she should love her baby sister, but she feels jealous of all the attention the baby gets. Mia wishes she had Mom and Dad to herself again.

Kirsty is Mia's friend

When I went to Mia's house to see the new baby, Mia kept trying to pull me away.

She said, "Play with me!" I said, "I want to play with baby Lola." Now Mia says I'm not her friend anymore!

Kirsty

Mia

Mia's story

Everyone comes over and makes a big deal about Lola. They don't notice me. I feel really left out.

I had Mom and Dad all to myself before baby Lola was born. Now I've got to share them. And it's not even a fair share. Lola gets loads of attention. I only get a teeny-weeny little bit.

I think Mom and Dad love baby Lola more than me. I think everyone loves her more than me! Sometimes I wish she had never been born.

What can Mia do?

Lots of kids feel jealous of a new baby. She can:

★ tell her mom and dad she feels left out
★ say she thinks they love the baby more than her
★ say she felt happier before

What Mia did

I told Mom and Dad I think they love the baby more than me. Mom and Dad said they love me just as much as ever. Now they love Lola, too.

There's plenty of love to go around. So when Lola's asleep, Mom or Dad have a special time with me. I'm OK with Kirsty playing with Lola, as long as she spends lots of time with me, too!

MY BABY BROTHER IS A NUISANCE!

Jade's baby brother Barney cries at night and wakes her up. Mom and Dad are tired. Her big sister Anna helps look after the baby. Jade thinks Barney's a nuisance.

Anna is Jade's big sister

Jade is angry all the time. She is angry with baby Barney, angry with Mom and Dad, and angry with me. I can't play with her much because I'm busy helping Mom look after baby Barney.

Anna

Jade's story

Everyone says how sweet baby Barney is.

I guess he is, sometimes, but mostly he's a nuisance! He cries all night and keeps everyone awake. Mom and Dad are always tired.

If he gives a little whimper, Anna rushes to look after him — even if we're in the middle of a game.

Now that he's crawling, he knocks over my toys and puts them in his mouth.

It takes ages to dress him and put him in his stroller every time we go out.

Babies need lots of care and attention. They take up a lot of time. She can:

★ tell her big sister she's angry because she thinks baby Barney is a nuisance

★ find ways she can help out with Barney and join in

What Jade did

I talked to Anna. She said she'd play with me more. Now I'm helping with Barney. I read him books and he tries to eat them. I put on his hat and he pulls it off.

I feed him and he blows his food at me. When I laugh at him, he giggles, too!

I WANT TO HELP!

When baby Alex was born, Gemma wanted to look after him.

Gemma's Mom's story

One day, baby Alex was crying in his bedroom and he suddenly stopped. I ran upstairs to find out why. Gemma had picked him up out of his crib.

I was really upset with her. She could have dropped him! She cried and said she was only trying to help.

I said, "I know you love Alex and want to help, but you are too young to do it all by yourself. You can help me and we'll look after Alex together."

WATCHING A BABY GROW

New babies can't do anything for themselves. They cry to get attention. Crying can mean, "I'm hungry! I've got a dirty diaper! I'm bored! I'm tired!" Sometimes it can mean, "Help! I don't feel good!"

Babies soon begin to smile. They get stronger and can sit up and hold things. You can read to them, play with them, and make them giggle. At six months, some babies begin to crawl. At twelve months, they may learn to walk. You can hold their hands to help them.

Babies can be lots of fun, but always ask an adult to help you play with a baby.

MY LITTLE SISTER ALWAYS GETS HER WAY!

Jesse's little sister Hanna has just learned to walk. She can say a few words. Jesse thinks his mom and dad expect him to do whatever she wants.

Aiden is Jesse's friend

Jesse always wants to come over and play at my house. He says he wants to get away from his baby sister. That's all right with me. Hanna ruins all our games!

Aiden

When baby Hanna was tiny, she was really sweet. I was the first person she smiled at!

She was funny when she fed herself. Everything got covered in food!

Now that she can toddle and say a few words, she gets away with everything!

I always have to do what Hanna wants. Mom and Dad say, "Give the toy to her, Jesse! Play with her, Jesse! She's only little."

If she cries, they say, "What have you done, Jesse?" when I haven't even done anything! I don't think she's sweet anymore!

Jesse

What can Jesse do?

It can be hard to love a baby brother or sister all the time. Jesse can:

* tell his mom and dad he wants to love Hanna
* say he doesn't think it's fair he is expected to do everything she wants
* say he is finding it hard to love her all the time

What Jesse did

I told Mom and Dad. They said Hanna is old enough to understand "No." When they say "No," she doesn't like it and makes a fuss. Mom distracts her and she quickly forgets it. Aiden comes over to my house again now that Hanna doesn't always get her own way.

WILL MY STEPDAD STILL LOVE ME?

Kayo's mom and stepdad are having a baby together. Her friend Padma is worried about her.

Padma

Padma is Kayo's friend

Kayo's been sad since she heard about the new baby. I thought she'd be happy.

She doesn't want to talk about it. I wish I knew why the new baby is making her sad.

Kayo's story

Mom and Dad are divorced. I live with Mom and my stepdad. I don't see my own dad very often, but I get along really well with my stepdad, Phil.

Phil doesn't have any other children, only me.

He says I'm his little girl.

I know my mom will always love me. But Phil's so happy he and Mom are having a baby, I'm afraid he won't love me when he's got a baby of his own.

What can Kayo do?

No one can help Kayo unless she tells them why she's sad. She can:

★ tell her friend Padma she thinks Phil won't love her when the baby arrives
★ tell her mom
★ tell Phil

What Kayo did

I told Padma and she said Phil wouldn't stop loving me. I told Mom and she said the same. Phil gave me a hug and he said the same! He said I would be a very special big sister. Now I'm looking forward to the new baby and I'm not sad anymore.

OUR NEW BABY

When Bonnie and Grace first heard their mom was going to have a new baby, they didn't know what to think.

Bonnie:
Mom and Dad were really excited about having a new baby. Grace and I weren't so sure!

Grace:
Babies need lots of looking after and they can't do much. I thought a new baby wouldn't be fun.

Bonnie:
Mom and Dad just expected us to be happy, so at first we pretended to be happy about our new baby brother or sister.

Grace:
But we couldn't fool Mom and Dad. They wanted to know what was going on.

Bonnie:
I told them I think having a baby will change everything. I like things just as they are. I said a baby will stop us from doing things together, like going swimming or going out for pizza.

Grace: Mom told us that the baby will change lots of things, but they can be good changes.

Bonnie: Dad said he'd make sure we still did the things we enjoy.

Grace: Mom said it wouldn't be long before the baby could join in, too.

Bonnie: When baby Pete was born, I thought he was really sweet.

Grace: I helped bathe and dress him. I thought he was noisy and smelly! But I liked the way he held onto my finger and made funny faces at me.

Bonnie: Now baby Pete is learning to walk. We make him laugh, and he can nearly say our names. Now we can't imagine not having him around.

GLOSSARY

Attention
You get attention when other people notice you and spend time with you.

Born
A baby is born when it is ready to leave its mother's womb and live separately from her.

Fair
A rule or a decision is fair when it is good for everyone involved.

Jealous
You feel jealous when you think someone else is getting more love and attention than you and it makes you unhappy.

Nuisance
Someone is a nuisance when they stop you from doing what you want to do, or when they are annoying.

Pretend
You pretend when you make other people believe something is true when it isn't really.

Scan
A photograph taken of an unborn baby in its mother's womb.

Share
You share when you tell or give things to other people and you don't keep things to yourself.

Womb
The part of a mother's body where a baby grows until it is ready to be born.

Worry
You worry when you feel troubled about something.

FURTHER INFORMATION

Books

Crist, James Ph.D. and Elizabeth Verdick. *Siblings: You're Stuck with Each Other, So Stick Together.* Free Spirit Publishing, 2016.

New Baby. Paragon Books, 2012.

Sornson, Bob. *Stand in My Shoes: Kids Learning About Empathy.* Love and Logic Press, 2013.

INDEX